W9-BDF-785

THE RULER OF THE SPRINGS

For Flora Mary Miranda Fisher — M. F.

To my three sisters — M. P.

Barefoot Books
Bradford Mill, 23 Bradford Street
West Concord, MA 01742

Barefoot Books
29/30 Fitzroy Square
London, W1T 6LQ

Text copyright © 2014 by Mary Finch
Illustrations copyright © 2014 by Martina Peluso
The moral rights of Mary Finch and Martina Peluso have been asserted

First published in the United States of America by Barefoot Books, Inc
and in Great Britain by Barefoot Books, Ltd in 2014
This paperback edition first published in 2021
All rights reserved

Graphic design by Katie Jennings Campbell, Asheville, NC, USA
Reproduction by B & P International, Hong Kong
Printed in China on 100% acid-free paper
This book was typeset in Bembo Infant, Foglighten and Mr Anteater
The illustrations were prepared in acrylic paint and graphite on paper
that is produced in Sicily near Mount Etna

Thank you to Year 2 at Thameside Primary School,
Reading, UK for all their careful reading

Sources:
"The Princess of the Springs: South American Folktale."
World of Tales. Web. May 2012.

ISBN 978-1-64686-338-9

British Cataloguing-in-Publication Data: a catalogue record
for this book is available from the British Library

Library of Congress Cataloging-in-Publication Data
is available under LCCN 2013031107

1 3 5 7 9 8 6 4 2

THE RULER OF THE SPRINGS

A Tale from Brazil

Retold by Mary Finch

Illustrated by Martina Peluso

Barefoot Books
step inside a story

CONTENTS

CHAPTER 1 – page 6
Princess Ibura

CHAPTER 2 – page 14
The Gold Palace

CHAPTER 3 – page 19
In Prison

CHAPTER 4 – page 35
The Lost Prince

CHAPTER 5 – page 42
The Giant of the Rain

CHAPTER 1

Princess Ibura

Once upon a time, when the world was young, the Moon Giant fell in love with the giantess who lived in the Great River. He built her a palace made of shells and silver and sparkling gems.

After a while, a baby girl was born to the Moon Giant and the Giantess of the Great River. Her eyes shone like the moon and she was as strong as the Great River. They called her Ibura, the Ruler of the Springs. She was the princess of all the springs, rivers and lakes in the land.

Ibura grew up to be beautiful, clever and wise. Her father lived in the night sky and she lived with her mother in the silver and shell palace. She wanted to stay there forever.

But the Sun Giant had seen the Ruler of the Springs in the waters of the rivers and streams as he crossed the sky every day. She was so beautiful that he fell in love with her. "Ah," he said. "That is the wife for me." He knocked on the door of the silver and shell palace and asked her to marry him.

"Oh, no," said Ibura. "I don't want to leave my mother."

But the Sun Giant had made up his mind. And being so strong and brave, he was used to getting his own way. Every day he asked Ibura to be his wife and live with him in his gold palace in the sky. Each time she said no, but each time he looked so sad that she began to care for him.

"Yes, I will marry you and live in your gold palace in the sky," she said at last, "but only if for three months of every year I can go home to my mother, the Giantess of the Great River, and the shell palace."

CHAPTER 2

The Gold Palace

So the Sun Giant and Ibura, the Ruler of the Springs, were married. They went to live in the gold palace in the sky. They were happy together.

The Sun Giant was kind and strong, but Ibura missed her mother. For three months each year she went home, and for those three months the Great River and the other rivers and lakes shone and sparkled with joy.

A baby son was born to Ibura and the Sun Giant. Ibura wanted to take him to the silver and shell palace and show him to the Giantess of the Great River. But the Sun Giant said she must leave their son with him.

"The prince must stay at home in the gold palace," he said. "He is too little to make the journey all the way down to the Great River with you."

Ibura was very sad. She loved her son and would miss him while she was gone. But she knew the Sun Giant would take care of him and she agreed that the prince should stay at the gold palace.

CHAPTER 3

In Prison

Ibura set off for the silver and shell palace, but when she arrived her mother was not there. The princess ran into every room. She called, "Mother, where are you?" But there was no answer.

The princess asked the fish in the Great River if they had seen her mother.

"No," they answered. "We haven't seen her."

The princess asked the sands on the seashore if they had seen her mother.

"No," they answered. "We haven't seen her."

She asked the yellow shells on the seashore if they had seen her mother.

"Ask the Giant of the Wind," they said. "He goes everywhere and knows everything."

The princess did not know what else to do. She went to the house of the Giant of the Wind. "Do you know where my mother is?" she asked him.

The Giant of the Wind promised he would look for the Giantess of the Great River. He blew over the hills and the forests and at last he came to the castle of the Giant of the Land.

The Giant of the Wind blew into every crack of the castle. In the deep dungeon he found Ibura's mother. The Giant of the Land had put the giantess in prison in the darkest part of his castle. He wanted to take the shell palace and the river for himself.

The Giant of the Wind went back to his house. He told the Ruler of the Springs that he had found her mother. He put the princess on his back and together they flew to the Giant of the Land's castle.

"Give me back my mother," said the Ruler of the Springs.

"No," said the Giant of the Land. "She is mine now and I will keep her."

"Then I will blow your house down!" said the Giant of the Wind. He blew and he blew and all of the doors crashed open, even the door of the deep dungeon.

The Giantess of the Great River was very happy to see her daughter. She had not liked the dark dungeon and longed to be in the open air again. Ibura led her mother outside and hugged her.

The princess and the Giantess of the Great River thanked the Giant of the Wind for his help. They went back to the shell palace. They had been away for more than three months.

"The Sun Giant will not know where I am. He will miss me," said Ibura. "And my son will miss me too. I must go home."

CHAPTER 4

The Lost Prince

The Sun Giant was very upset when the Ruler of the Springs did not come home after three months. Instead of looking for Ibura, he married another wife. The new wife was jealous of the little prince. She sent him away, out into the sky.

But the cook felt sorry for the little prince. He saw how lost and lonely he was out in the clouds. The cook took the prince back to the palace and hid him in the kitchen. The prince played with the dogs and ate the scraps that the kind cook gave him. The little prince was so dirty that nobody knew who he was.

When the Ruler of the Springs arrived back at the palace of the Sun Giant, she called out for her son. The little prince was not there. One of the palace servants began to cry and told the princess how the new wife had sent him away.

"Where is he?" the princess asked.

"I don't know," said the poor servant.

"Then we must find him at once," said the princess. And she ran through the gardens and the palace calling for her little boy, but it did no good.

The princess was so sad that she went back to the Great River to be with her mother. There she wept and wept and wept for forty days.

And as she wept, her tears made the Great River flood into the sea, and the sea rose so high that it covered the gold palace of the Sun Giant.

For forty days the palace of the Sun Giant, and everyone inside, was covered by the sea. The Sun Giant could not shine on the earth and the land was dark.

CHAPTER 5

The Giant of the Rain

The prince was very sad too. He missed his mother, the Ruler of the Springs, and he didn't want to stay in the palace kitchen with just the dogs and the cook for friends and scraps for food.

He left the palace and set off into the clouds where he began to cry. His tears washed his face clean and fell all the way down to the earth.

Ibura felt the tears dropping around her. She looked up and saw her son crying. She rushed up into the sky as fast as she could to bring him home.

She picked the prince up and hugged him. He told her how the kind cook had hidden him, but how he missed her and was always hungry.

Then the Ruler of the Springs dried her tears, took the little prince by the hand and went home to the silver and shell palace and the Giantess of the Great River. There she stayed and she didn't go back to the Sun Giant.

The little prince grew up to be the Giant of the Rain. When rain falls on the earth in the rainy season it is him, dropping tears like he did when his mother was far away and he was sad and all alone. And the thirsty land welcomes the rain, the crops grow tall and strong, and the Ruler of the Springs makes the rivers and lakes sparkle with joy.